WILLIAM SHAKESPEARE

THE TEMPEST

RETOLD BY Ann Keay Beneduce

ILLUSTRATED BY Gennady Spirin

PHILOMEL BOOKS NEW YORK

For Sandra Jordan, who had the dream.—A.K.B.

In memory of my grandmother.—G.S.

Text copyright © 1996 by Ann Keay Beneduce
Illustrations copyright © 1996 by Gennady Spirin
All rights reserved. This book, or parts thereof, may not be reproduced
in any form without permission in writing from the publisher,
Philomel Books, a division of The Putnam & Grosset Group,
200 Madison Avenue, New York, NY 10016. Philomel Books,
Reg. U.S. Pat. & Tm. Off. Published simultaneously in Canada
Printed in Hong Kong by South China Printing Co. (1988) Ltd.
The text is set in Bernhard Modern.

Library of Congress Cataloging-in-Publication Data
Beneduce, Ann. The Tempest / by William Shakespeare;
retold by Ann Keay Beneduce; illustrated by Gennady Spirin. p.   cm.
1. Shakespeare, William, 1564-1616. Tempest—Juvenile fiction.
[1. Shakespeare, William, 1564-1616—Adaptations.] I. Spirin,
Gennadii. II. Shakespeare, William, 1564-1616. Tempest.
III. Title. PR2878.T4B46   1996   94-33357   CIP   AC
ISBN 0-399-22764-4
1 3 5 7 9 10 8 6 4 2

Be not afeard; the isle is full of noises,
Sounds and sweet airs, that give delight and hurt not.
Sometimes a thousand twangling instruments
Will hum about mine ears....

Once upon a time there was an enchanted island, a green and lovely place, set in the great sea that lies between Europe and Africa. The air was filled with the sounds of music and the fragrance of flowers. There in a large cave on the island lived an old magician, Prospero, and his beautiful daughter, Miranda. They were the only human beings on the island, though there were other creatures—Ariel, a friendly but mischievous spirit, and his band of goblins, imps and other magical creatures. And there was the evil Caliban.

Prospero and Miranda had first found Caliban—an ugly, inhuman monster—wandering in the woods. They took him home, taught him to speak, and treated him kindly. But Caliban remained evil in spite of all they did. One day he even tried to harm the gentle Miranda! After that, to punish him, Prospero gave Caliban all the heaviest work to do.

When Caliban was lazy, Ariel, the magician's helper, would send his imps and goblins to trip him and pinch him and goad him back to work. Ariel loved teasing the monster. But Caliban, in return, hated both Ariel and Prospero with a deadly passion.

One morning, Miranda and her father stood on the grassy hill outside of their cave. Suddenly they saw a fine ship just offshore—the first ship Miranda had ever seen. But though the weather on the island was fair, a tempest seemed to be overtaking the ship. The dark, rain-laden sky above it was streaked with lightning, which danced like fire along the wooden beams that held the sails and threatened to set the whole ship aflame. Towering waves tossed the ship wildly from side to side. Miranda could hear the shouts and cries of the terrified sailors and see the passengers, one of whom leaped over the side to almost certain death as she watched.

"Oh, Father," cried Miranda. "Is this some magic storm that you have called up to drown these poor creatures? Look! Their ship is being dashed to pieces! Besides you, these are the first fellow humans I have ever seen. Have pity on them!"

Her father didn't take his eyes off the ship. "Don't be afraid, Miranda," he said. "Yes, I have called up this storm by my magic. But I have sent Ariel to be sure that everyone on board will be saved. Even the ship will not be harmed. I know it seems strange to hear me say this, but you must believe that I have done all this for your sake, my dear child."

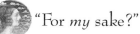 "For *my* sake?"

"Yours. Tell me, do you remember anything at all from the time before we came to this island twelve years ago?"

"Almost nothing," she replied.

"Then let me tell you." The old magician told her he had once been the rich and powerful Duke of Milan. A wise and just ruler, he was known as a great scholar. Miranda was a princess and his only heir, as her mother had died when she born. But even a wise man can make a mistake. Prospero made the error of appointing his brother, Antonio, to deal with the matters of governing Milan, while he buried himself in his beloved books.

"I trusted Antonio," he went on, "but he betrayed me. With the help of the King of Naples, Antonio stole my dukedom, and set you and me adrift on the open sea in a small boat. You were only three years old. We would surely have died, but for the kindness of one of the king's counselors. He stocked our poor little boat with food and clothing and even my books of magic. Luckily, we were cast ashore here on this island. The rest you know."

Miranda shook her head in amazement. "Why did Antonio not just have us killed?"

"He dared not," said Prospero. "We were much beloved by our people. But that was a dozen years ago. My chief delight since then has been in teaching you, Miranda, and you have been a very good student."

"But, Father," she asked him, "why have you used your magic to raise this terrible tempest?"

"Because my enemies, the King of Naples and my brother, Antonio, are on that ship!

Soon they will be cast ashore on this island. Now, at last, I can take my revenge on them! But enough—I have made you tired with all of this."

Prospero touched her gently with his magic wand. Instantly, Miranda sank to the grass and fell into a deep sleep. As he turned away, Ariel flew to his side.

"Well, my brave spirit," said Prospero, "how have you performed your task?"

"Perfectly," replied Ariel. "The ship is safely in harbor, though out of sight; and the sailors are asleep below deck. The passengers are safe, too, on various parts of the island. The king is grieving because he saw his son, Prince Ferdinand, jump overboard. He is sure he has perished. Ferdinand, too, is grieving. He thinks his father and all on the ship must have drowned!"

"That's my good Ariel! Well done! Now bring young Prince Ferdinand here."

"More work, Prospero? You had promised me my liberty after twelve years. Now it is twelve years to the day!"

"Not quite yet, Ariel. But if you do my bidding in this, I promise I will soon set you free."

"Well, then, I'll obey you a little longer," said Ariel. "I'll bring Ferdinand here now." And away he flew, singing a strange song.

Full fathom five thy father lies;
Of his bones are coral made;
Those are pearls that were his eyes;
Nothing of him that doth fade,
But doth suffer a sea-change
Into something rich and strange.
Sea-nymphs hourly ring his knell;
Hark! Now I hear them: Ding-dong bell.

Poor Ferdinand was still sitting where Ariel had left him, on the other side of the island, deep in sorrow. But Ariel's song, which seemed to him to be about his father's drowning, roused him. Following where the voice led him, through forests and over hills, he came to where Prospero and Miranda were sitting under the shade of a large tree.

Miranda had never seen a man before, except her own father.

"Look, Father!" she exclaimed. "What a beautiful creature! Surely it is a spirit, is it not?"

"No, dear girl, it is merely human—it eats and sleeps and has senses just like ours," her father said to her.

Ferdinand was as surprised and charmed by Miranda as she was by him. Indeed, he thought she must be the goddess of the island, which he began to think was enchanted.

The two young people fell into earnest conversation. As the minutes stretched into hours, it was clear that it was love at first sight between them. But could Prospero trust Ferdinand? After all, he was the son of Prospero's enemy, the treacherous King of Naples. Prospero decided he should test Ferdinand, to be sure he really loved Miranda. So he pretended to think that the prince was a spy.

"I know who you are," he said, "and I have a fit punishment for a traitor."

"Have pity, sir!" Miranda begged her father. "I am sure this man is true and honorable!"

"Silence!" said her father. "You think there are no other men as fine as he, because you have seen only him and me—and that beast Caliban. I tell you that most men are much better than he, as he is better than Caliban!"

Of course, he said this only to test his daughter's feelings about the prince.

"I have no wish to see a better man than this one," Miranda replied.

11

Prospero was not satisfied. "Bring these heavy logs of wood out of the forest and pile them neatly outside this dwelling," he told the prince. "And finish this task by sunset." He knew this would be almost impossible to do. Ferdinand set to work with a will. But kings' sons are not used to this kind of work, so Ferdinand was soon very tired.

Prospero watched him for a few minutes, then went into his study. Then, making himself invisible, he watched and listened to the lovers as they talked.

"Let me help you," he heard Miranda say to the prince. "My father won't know the difference. He is in his study and will be busy there for hours. You look weary."

"No, noble lady," replied Ferdinand. "When you are here, I feel fresh as morning. Oh, Miranda, I have known many women, but none as perfect as you."

"I have never seen another man but you and my father," said Miranda, "but I cannot imagine any companion I could want except yourself."

"My dearest Miranda, in my own land I am a prince. Or, if my dear father has perished in the storm, I am already the king. But here, I am willing for love of you to try to please your father."

"Do you really love me, then?" asked Miranda.

"Beyond anything in the world," declared the prince.

Now Prospero, hearing this, was convinced that Ferdinand was sincere. He walked, still invisible, to another part of the island, making plans for his disloyal brother, Antonio, and the King of Naples. First, he and Ariel gathered together in the forest all those of the royal party who had been cast ashore during the tempest. He himself remained unseen. Then, with his magic, he spread before the exhausted, hungry group the most magnificent feast that could be imagined: a table set with silver and rich linens and laden with roasts and sweetmeats, fruits and wines. Dancers performed their nimble art to music played by an invisible orchestra.

Delighted, the voyagers were just about to eat when all at once, with a roll of drums and a puff of smoke—*poof!*—the banquet vanished into thin air. On the empty table before the disappointed group appeared Ariel in the form of an old harpy. Looking straight at the king and Antonio, the harpy spoke to them, reminding them of what they had done to Prospero and Miranda. It warned them that they would soon be punished for their sins. Then it vanished as completely as the banquet.

Guilty and ashamed of their evil deeds, the king and Antonio were terrified. What further punishments were in store for them? Would they ever leave the island alive? Most frightening, they found they could not move. Some enchantment held them and their attendants where they were, as firmly as if they were chained prisoners.

Now the magician returned to his cave, where he had left his daughter and Ferdinand a little earlier. They were still talking. "Will you be my bride?" he heard Ferdinand ask Miranda. "I will," she replied. At this, Prospero made himself visible, and said to the young prince,

"If I have been too harsh, you have taken it very well. I felt I had to test your love before I could give you the richest gift I have—my dear daughter. Oh, Ferdinand, don't smile if I boast of her—you will find that she deserves my praise and even more."

"I do believe it, sir," replied Ferdinand.

"She will be yours," said the magician. "And now, let's celebrate! Ariel, sweet spirit, where are you?"

"Here, my master. What do you wish?"

"You and your band of spirits have worthily performed the disappearing banquet! Now I must ask you to arrange an even more marvelous entertainment for my daughter and her husband-to-be. I have promised them this—can you do it?"

"In the twinkle of an eye, sir," said Ariel, flying off.

Almost immediately, the sky opened, and down floated Iris, the rainbow goddess. Then came Ceres, goddess of the harvest. Next, and most important of all, came Juno, the wife of the great Roman god Jupiter, singing to the young couple. Ceres, too, sang a song of good wishes. Then Iris called on her dancers.

Juno's Blessing

Honour, riches, marriage-blessing,
Long continuance, and increasing,
Hourly joys be still upon you!
Juno sings her blessings on you.

Ceres's Blessing

Vines with clustering bunches growing
Plants with goodly burthen bowing;
Spring come to you at the farthest
In the very end of harvest!
Scarcity and want shall shun you;
Ceres's blessing so is on you.

Iris Calls the Dancers

Come, temperate nymphs, and help to celebrate
A contract of true love; be not too late.
Come sunburnt sicklemen, of August weary,
Come hither from the furrow and be merry.

As they watched the graceful dancers, Ferdinand turned to Miranda and said, "I think I must be in Paradise!"

But, suddenly, in the midst of the festivities, Ariel appeared and said something to Prospero that the others could not hear. The old magician frowned and raised one hand. Immediately, there was a strange, hollow noise—and then the dancers and the entire pageant disappeared! Prospero turned to Ferdinand, saying, "I'm sorry to have to cut our celebration short." And he went on, speaking a little strangely.

Prospero's Speech

Our revels now are ended. These our actors,
As I foretold you, were all spirits and
Are melted into air, into thin air:
And, like the baseless fabric of this vision,
The cloud-capped towers, the gorgeous palaces,
The solemn temples, the great globe itself,
Yea, all which it inherits, shall dissolve
And, like this insubstantial pageant faded,
Leave not a rack behind. We are such stuff
As dreams are made of, and our little life
Is rounded with a sleep.

Then, seeing Ferdinand's bewildered expression, Prospero stopped, saying, "But, bear with me . . . I am upset. My old brain is troubled. Wait for me in my study, you and Miranda, while I go for a little walk to still my mind."

"We'll do that, sir. We wish you peace."

The old magician smiled briefly as the two young people walked inside the cave together, already deep in conversation. Then he turned to Ariel, who said, "Dear master, I'm sorry to spoil this happy moment, but I have very bad news. The monster Caliban is on his way here to murder you! He has found two men from the ship wandering in the forest and has tricked them into joining in his evil plan."

"That Caliban! A born devil! All my kindness has been wasted on him, alas!" exclaimed Prospero. "But don't worry, my good Ariel. I have an idea for dealing with Caliban and his murderous fellows. We will teach them a lesson, with the help of a little magic! Where did you say you had left them?"

"Master, I have already led them into the swamp, and their clothes are all covered with foul-smelling mud."

"Good work! Now, dear Ariel, please bring them here."

"No sooner said than done, master," said Ariel, who flew off and quickly returned, leading Caliban and Trincolo and Stephano, his accomplices in crime, to where Prospero stood waiting.

The sound of a hunter's horn was heard. Immediately, a crowd of elves and spirits, disguised as hunters and hounds, burst out of the woods and began to chase the three villains.

"Hey, Mountain, hey!" cried Prospero to one of the spirits. "After the rascals!"

"Silver! There he goes, Silver! Get him!" called Ariel.

"Fury, Fury! There, Tyrant, there! Hark, hark!" Prospero urged each of the spirits on, as Caliban, Trincolo and Stephano fled, roaring with terror.

Laughing, Prospero and Ariel returned to the clearing in front of the magician's cave. "Well done, my clever Ariel," said Prospero. "What time is it now?"

"Six o'clock, sir."

"Well, a great deal has happened since I conjured up that tempest this morning! There is just a little more work to be done before the day is ended. Your spirits will catch and punish those rascals, I am sure. Now where are the king and his comrades?"

"They are still where they were after the banquet, held prisoners by your magic."

"Go fetch them, Ariel—bring them here."

While he waited for Ariel to come back with the prisoners, Prospero drew a circle on the grass before him. His magic had brought all his enemies into his grasp. At last he could take sweet revenge, as he had long planned.

Soon Ariel reappeared with Prospero's brother, Antonio, and Ferdinand's father, the King of Naples, as well as their attendants. The prisoners stepped within the magic circle Prospero had drawn, and stood there trembling, unable to escape. But Prospero was not yet ready to announce their fate to them. He had another surprise planned for them. He called on his helper for one more service: "Ariel, please bring me the hat and sword that hang in my cave."

"I'll be back in one heartbeat!" said Ariel, and he soon returned, carrying with him the hat and sword. He handed them to Prospero, who donned the plumed hat, seized his sword and, with a flourish, tossed aside his star-strewn magician's cloak.

"Behold, sir, the rightful Duke of Milan!" he said to the amazed king. "I am Prospero. I embrace thee—*and I pardon thee!*"

"Are you really Prospero? Or just his ghost that I have dreamed up in a fit of madness?" The king fell to his knees. "Either way, I give you back your dukedom and beg your forgiveness for my wrongs. . . . But Prospero was set adrift to die twelve years ago. How could he still be living and be here?"

"It is a long, strange story, and I will tell it to you later," replied Prospero, "but first let me speak with my brother, with whom I have no further quarrel, since you have given me back my dukedom. And then I want to give you something in return."

"Alas, nothing you can give me will mean anything to me," said the king, "since I lost my son, Ferdinand, in the tempest this morning."

"I understand your sorrow," said Prospero, "but still, I have something of value for you. Please look in here now." So saying, he flung aside the curtain from in front of his cave—and there sat Ferdinand and Miranda, playing a game of chess! Overwhelmed with joy to find each other still alive, father and son embraced. Then the king turned to meet his son's companion.

"Is she a goddess?" he asked, just as Ferdinand had.

"No, sir, though she is lovely enough to be one, I agree," replied the prince. "And to my delight, she has agreed to be your future daughter-in-law."

In the meantime, Miranda was looking around at the assembled noblemen in amazement.

"How beautiful they are!" she cried. "What a wonderful new world I am about to enter, that has such people in it!"

"Well, I see I have no further need for magic!" exclaimed Prospero. "My daughter's happiness is assured; my dukedom is restored. I have all I could wish for now. I'll bury my wand, drown my books of spells—and give up my conjurer's art forever!"

27

The rest of the day and evening passed in a flurry of plans for the voyage back to Naples and the royal wedding, as well as for Prospero's triumphant return to Milan. Ferdinand and Miranda were so much in love and so happy together that the hardest heart would have had to melt in their presence.

So it came about that Prospero declared that the brutish Caliban was not to be punished but just left on the island alone, as he wished. He pardoned Caliban's co-conspirators, too.

And that merry spirit Ariel was set free at last, having served his master faithfully for his appointed term. But, since Prospero had given up magic, Ariel offered to use his own enchantments to bring the ship safely across the sea and back to Naples, which he did the next day, flying alongside the ship and singing all the way.

Ariel's Song

Where the bee sucks, there suck I:
In a cowslip's bell I lie;
There I couch when owls do cry.
On the bat's back I do fly
After summer merrily.
Merrily, merrily shall I live now
Under the blossom that hangs on the bough.

About THE TEMPEST

This delightful play was written toward the end of Shakespeare's life, probably in 1610, and it is impossible to read it without finding many things that seem to refer to the playwright himself. For instance, at the end, when Prospero looks at what he has achieved—his dukedom restored to him, his respected position in society confirmed, his daughter's future happiness assured—he decides it is time to give up his magical art. Could Shakespeare have meant this also as his farewell to the theater? We can never know the answer to this question, of course, but it is tempting to look for parallels.

Some of the ideas for *The Tempest* came from contemporary reports of adventures Shakespeare had surely read, such as an account of the wreck of a ship, the *Sea Venture*, on an island somewhere in the Bermudas said to be inhabited by strange monsters. Tales of cannibals and other such creatures were told by returning explorers; the name Caliban was an anagram of the word cannibal. The playwright did not have to go far afield to find a tale of political intrigue, as clashes between rival city-states in Italy and elsewhere were common in those days. As for magic, people in Shakespeare's day still respected its power, and fairies, elves and other spirits were popularly believed to exist. The *masque* or celebration, with its Roman goddesses, was a fashionable feature of many plays at the time, reflecting the excitement over the rediscovery of the culture and art of ancient Greece and Rome that took place during the Renaissance.

In this play, Shakespeare holds a mirror to our own world and its problems. As the drama unfolds, many philosophical points are raised that are as worthy of consideration today as in Shakespeare's time. Central to the story is the issue of justice versus revenge—an issue still very much alive today. Love for his daughter forces the old magician to reconsider his long-planned punishment of his enemies, whom he has completely in his power. Prospero wisely decides that justice—the return to him of his usurped dukedom—and the repentance of the evildoers are better than revenge. So good triumphs over evil, and love conquers all.

About William Shakespeare

Born in 1564 in Stratford-upon-Avon, England, William Shakespeare was the son of a simple tradesman and glovemaker. He went on to become the greatest playwright in the English language, not only of his own time, but probably of all time.

Married at the age of eighteen to Anne Hathaway, he may have worked for a while in his father's trade, then as a tutor or a schoolmaster. In 1587 a theatrical group called The Queen's Men performed in Stratford, and it is thought that Shakespeare returned with them to London. He soon established himself there as an actor and play-wright. During the years 1590–92 his three plays, the *Henry IV* trilogy, were performed, bringing him immediate acclaim. His innate love of words and his capacity for hard work enabled him to produce in his rather short lifetime thirty-four more plays—historical dramas, comedies and tragedies —which are still performed, studied and admired all over the world today. In 1602 he bought a house and a large piece of land in Stratford, his birthplace, which he had left as a penniless actor only fifteen years earlier. Now he was one of the richest and most respected men in the town.

Shakespeare died in 1616, on what is believed to be his birthday, April 23, at his home in Stratford.

About this Retelling of THE TEMPEST

This book is intended to offer young readers a very brief, but inviting glimpse of the stage itself—and of the enchantment that awaits them when, later on, they can see a full-length performance of this magnificent play.

In converting Shakespeare's classic fantasy into an illustrated story for young readers and listeners, some of the characters and complex action of the play had to be omitted because of limitations of space. And some of what was kept has been drastically altered. In particular, the language, so beautiful but so difficult in the original, has been simplified; archaisms have been removed and confusing historical references deleted. For all these transgressions, the reteller humbly apologizes. While painful to those who know and love the play in its entirety, these revisions seemed necessary in order to ensure that no barriers stood between the young readers and their enjoyment of the story itself.

The action of the retold text follows Shakespeare's version fairly faithfully. However, Act I, Scene 1, a "close-up" of the tempest-tossed ship, has been omitted, though in a real performance it provides an exciting beginning. Our story starts with Act I, Scene 2, where we meet Prospero, Miranda, Ariel and Caliban and see the ship and its imperiled passengers. Act II, Scene 1, containing a subplot in which Sebastian and Antonio plan to murder the King of Naples and his counsellor Gonzalo, has been deleted, along with Act II, Scene 2, and Act III, Scene 2, in which Caliban's rebellious plot to murder Prospero starts to take shape. (The amusing scene showing how this plot was foiled is included, however.)

In so small a space it was impossible to retain all the marvelous poetry of the original, but brief excerpts of some of the most famous verses are included to give those who are meeting Shakespeare for the first time here some sense of the magic of this great master's writing.

About Gennady Spirin

Gennady Spirin was born in a small city near Moscow on December 25, 1948. A graduate of the Strogonov Academy of Fine Arts, he is noted for his beautiful illustrations, meticulously researched and exquisitely executed in pencil and watercolor. His work has brought him international renown as well as many awards, including the Gold Medal of the Society of Illustrators, the Golden Apple of the Bratislava International Biennale of children's book illustration, First Prize for Illustration at the Barcelona International Children's Book Fair, and the Premio Grafico at the Bologna Children's Book Fair; his book *Gulliver's Adventures in Lilliput* was chosen one of the 10 Best Illustrated Books of the Year by *The New York Times Book Review*. Gennady Spirin came to the United States in 1991, and now lives in Princeton, New Jersey.

About Ann Keay Beneduce

Formerly an editor of children's books, Ann Beneduce now devotes herself to writing books for children and young people. She has also translated a number of books from French to English. In addition to *The Tempest*, she has retold several other classic tales, including *Gulliver's Adventures in Lilliput*, which was illustrated by Gennady Spirin.